INFILTRATE
RETRIBUTION

D1026158

INFILTRATE
RETRIBUTION

JUDITH GRAVES

ORCA BOOK PUBLISHERS

Library and Archives Canada Cataloguing in Publication

Graves, Judith, author
Infiltrate / Judith Graves.
(Retribution)

Issued in print and electronic formats.
ISBN 978-1-4598-0723-5 (softcover).—ISBN 978-1-4598-1488-2 (PDF).—
ISBN 978-1-4598-1489-9 (EPUB)

I. Title. II. Series: Retribution (Victoria, B.C.)
PS8613.R3827154 2017   jc813'.6   c2017-900844-7
c2017-900845-5

First published in the United States, 2017
Library of Congress Control Number: 2017933014

Summary: In this installment of the high-interest Retribution series,
Raven goes undercover to find the link between a pharmaceutical
company and a wave of teen suicides.

*Orca Book Publishers is dedicated to preserving the environment and has
printed this book on Forest Stewardship Council® certified paper.*

Orca Book Publishers gratefully acknowledges the support for its publishing
programs provided by the following agencies: the Government of Canada
through the Canada Book Fund and the Canada Council for the Arts,
and the Province of British Columbia through the BC Arts Council
and the Book Publishing Tax Credit.

Edited by Tanya Trafford
Cover image by iStock.com
Author photo by Curtis Comeau

ORCA BOOK PUBLISHERS
www.orcabook.com

Printed and bound in Canada.

20 19 18 17 • 4 3 2 1

*To Brenda—my sister,
cheerleader and best friend.*

in·fil·trate (\in-ˈfil-ˌtrāt)
verb
to enter or become established in gradually or unobtrusively, usually for subversive purposes

ONE

The monsters are back.

I run for the hall closet. I almost don't fit, but I push and shove and squish myself inside. I lean on stinking clothes and junk piled nearly as tall as I am. My breathing is nothing but harsh pants. Too loud. They'll hear me. Find me. I cup a hand over my face to muffle the sounds.

This wasn't my smartest move. Our apartment is only on the second floor. I should have climbed out my bedroom window and jumped the few feet to the ground. Waited until it was safe to return. I've done it before.

But I'd thought the monsters were gone for good. They'd promised. Now I'm pretty much trapped, and they know my hiding places.

Footsteps pound down the hallway.

"Where'd you get to, little bird?" one low voice asks. It sounds like my father, but I know better.

My whole body trembles.

"Don't you want to see what we've got for you?" This voice sounds so much like my mother's. But it's rougher. Desperate.

I don't want to see what they have for me. Nothing good ever comes from the monsters.

Heavy thuds. Close. Loud.

My heart knocks hard in my ears. I burrow deep into the mounds of dirty clothes and drag what I can over my head. If I'm small enough, quiet enough, just maybe...

The door jerks open and light floods the closet, seeping through the gaps between sweaters and ripped jeans to edge my skin in a golden glow. They'll see me for sure. A scream sticks in my throat. I stay absolutely still. I hold my breath. I hold on to nothing *and pretend I'm not here—I'm somewhere else. I'm someone else. A queen in a castle. A wizard working a spell. A girl safe in her own home.*

The comforting weight of the clothes is suddenly gone. I gasp at the painful grip on my arm. It's all too real. And so am I.

No getting away this time.

"There she is, there's our little Raven." The monsters close in. They rip me apart.

I let the scream out then. And another. And another.

I jolted awake and slid out of bed, disoriented. The dream lingered, the terror sticking close like an old frenemy. I pulled on some clothes and decided it was time to climb. The fact that it was 4:30 AM didn't matter.

Climbing kept the monsters where they belonged.

In my nightmares.

TWO

I scaled the steel underbelly of the Burrard Street Bridge. A foggy haze blanketed the churning water below. I planted my feet on the rusted beam I'd been navigating for the last ten minutes and caught my breath. I released my hold on the taut suspension cable to take a quick swipe at the moisture collecting on my top lip.

It hadn't been raining when I set out for a bit of soloing, but hey, this was Vancouver. In the fall. It rained at least once a day, no ifs, ands or buts.

Most people just weren't climbing bridges during the downpour, trying to forget what should have been forgotten long ago.

A thrum of wings in my ear had me ducking out of range as a pigeon swooped by my head to perch on an opposing beam. Beady black eyes fixed on mine.

"Waiting to see if I fall?" I made my way forward, careful to avoid the pools of water building in the beam's ruts and cavities. Last thing I needed was an unwanted dip in False Creek. "You never know. I might surprise you, Beady Eyes, and just fly on out of here. My name is Raven, after all."

The pigeon tilted its head, puffed its feathers and cooed smugly. I could almost hear its thoughts. *A girl who can fly. Riiight.*

Yeah, that scenario wasn't too likely. I was no superhero with the ability to fly or melt things with my mind. But I was still about 98 percent certain I'd make it up the support tower. I'd plotted my route carefully, and the only tricky stretch left was straight ahead. I had random patches of scaffolding to contend with, thanks to certain sections of the bridge being under construction.

I reached for a pipe overhead and swung through a gap in the crisscross of steel pipes, releasing my grip just as my feet made contact with the waterlogged wooden platform. My trail-running shoes hydroplaned across the surface, and I dropped to my knees. They took a beating at the heavy impact, but if I hadn't, my momentum would have propelled me over the edge.

I sucked in a breath. That had been way, waaay too close for comfort.

At my back, Beady Eyes cooed, sounding vaguely disappointed.

I began to climb the tower. It was easier on this side without all the scaffolding and work-tool clutter. Funny— the construction workers were tied in when they worked at this height, and here I was, moving past all their various rigging without a care. "Bye-bye, birdy."

I never did like pigeons much. I'd had far too many run-ins with them during my climbs. You knew those birds were aiming for you when they had to do their business. They were strategic poopers, precise aerial bombers, almost always hitting their targets with goopy, stinking payloads.

Finally I reached the top, without a single misstep or bird-dropping situation. *Success.* Of course, the rain started to slow the second I was out of danger. I sat on the concrete railing, legs dangling over the edge, and watched the morning sun begin to burn through the cloud cover. The bridge, built sometime in the 1930s, stood about eighty feet above the waterline, with impressive art-deco towers. It was one of my favorite structures to climb, even if the recent construction took away some of the true climb. I loved that the city wasn't giving up on the old bridge and was doing the required upkeep.

Just because something was old school didn't mean it wasn't worthy of respect.

I thought of my houseboat, a clunker from the '80s, but still my safe haven, my home and my escape plan. *Big Daddy* had been moored for the last few years, but I kept it seaworthy in case I needed to make a clean break. So far I'd been lucky. But I knew, better than most, that your life could get swept up in a squall when you least expected it.

Actually, the last few weeks had been all about changing course. Adjusting and figuring out how to live this new life I had going. My old boss, Diesel, was no longer calling the shots. He'd led the car-theft ring I'd worked for. A criminal. And yet he was the man who'd kept me off the streets, given me a specific skill set—a purpose. But then he'd betrayed my trust. He'd been better than family, or so I'd thought, but when I'd learned the truth, what he was capable of, I'd exposed him for the monster he was. Life as I'd known it had changed, forever. No more stealing cars, no more high pressure or constant threats. Just infinite possibilities.

I'd learned that that could be scarier than having no possibilities at all. Having options meant more ways to screw up. With only myself to blame if things went south. Without the distractions of living at the warehouse with the other chop-shop kids, I had to focus on my future. Decide what I wanted out of my life. Who I was willing to trust and who now trusted me, like the kids who contacted Team Retribution for help. The team—Jo, Jace, Bentley and me—was the only thing keeping me going right now, although it caused a new kind of stress.

With new kinds of complications.

Like Emmett, the guy I was seriously crushing on. He was a cop's kid, and in his case—it was cliché but oh so true— the apple hadn't fallen far from the tree.

He wanted to know more about me—
where I lived, for example, or where my
parents were, or why I took such risks
with the team. The more I deflected, the
more he dug in his heels. He'd figured a
few things out, but still had questions I
couldn't answer. Not yet.

The nightmare flashed through my
mind. Maybe not ever. How could someone
like him understand the way I'd lived?
What I'd done? What I continued to do?
All his life Emmett had been surrounded
by good. Protected. He still believed in the
system while I bucked it at every turn.

I squinted down at the street below.
The fog had thickened, surrounding the
city in a heavy mist. With visibility this
bad, I decided to stay on the up side of the
bridge and make my way home. Swinging
a leg over the railing, I hopped down onto
one of the narrow walkways.

A scuffling sound drew my attention.
I spun to see a girl about my age on the

opposite side of the bridge. She was standing on the railing, one arm wrapped tightly around the section's support beam. With her back to me, she was unaware of my presence. Her arms were trembling, and no wonder—she was wearing just a tank top and shorts.

Must have been freezing up there, exposed to the wind.

I fought the urge to call out. I didn't want to startle her. My feet moved swift and silent on the damp concrete. I had to get closer and see what was going on.

A few steps in, my heart began to jackhammer behind my ribs. No way was this a fellow climber out for an early-morning challenge. The girl was off balance, in more ways than one. She stared down into the fog like it had all the answers.

What if she was planning to…

"Hey, what are you doing up there?" The words tumbled from my mouth.

The girl shot me a quick look, then stepped farther from the support beam. Wobbled on the railing.

"Don't! Please don't," I pleaded as I charged down the bridge at full speed.

But instead of leaping off the bridge to certain death, the girl crouched, placed her hands on the railing and hopped back down to the bridge's concrete surface.

She turned and sprinted into the fog.

"Wait! Are you okay? I just want to make sure you're all right." I slowed to a stop when the fog swallowed her form completely.

THREE

I kicked off my shoes and tugged my hoodie over my head. Went to drape it over a chair to dry, but it fell with a lifeless thud to the wood floor.

I let out a sigh.

Adapt and Overcome was a great motto to have when I was in the zone, scaling buildings and vaulting into space, but on *Big Daddy* I liked things in order. Consistent. So I was mighty mad when, as I tried to slip quietly into the cabin, my shin met the hard corner of the heavy wood chair that had no business being in the middle of the room.

"What the…" I grumbled under my breath and sidestepped around the chair. That's the thing about living on a small boat. Its cave-like darkness. Maybe I needed to invest in some string lights to provide a bit of a glow. I crept closer to the wall, searching for the light switch, and stubbed my toe on another piece of furniture not where it should be.

I swore, hopping on one foot as the pain traveled up my leg and straight to my stomach. *Ugh*. A broken toe was all I needed. And after my nightmare and what I'd seen or almost seen this morning—a girl thinking of jumping off a bridge to end her life—my tolerance for drama was at an all-time low.

The overhead lights popped on.

"And here I thought you had ninja skills." Jo's voice was thick with sleep and her usual feisty attitude.

"I should have known." Occasionally Jo crashed at my place when she needed to keep her head down. Get even further off grid than she normally was. Not that many could track a girl who'd spent years on the streets, learning to blend. To be invisible.

Survive.

Jo and I had an open-door policy now that I'd personally seen to vastly improving her previously limited B-and-E skills. She would never need a key to open a standard deadbolt again.

"I thought I told you to stop moving stuff." Since Jo was already awake, I spent a few seconds putting everything back in its proper place. One bonus of a liveaboard—small boat equals easy-peasy cleanup. Besides the tiny galley kitchen, *Big Daddy* had one narrow stateroom and a bench in the cabin that pulled out into a berth. Where Jo was currently sleeping.

"OCD much?" Jo snorted, pulling the comforter back over her head.

I immediately yanked it off. "GED ever?"

Jo groaned. "Not this again. I'm not going to your stupid school, or Jace's, or any education institution with teachers and doors and walls." She propped herself up on an elbow. "You know they practice lockdowns in schools and trap everyone inside, right?"

I frowned. "That's not how it works—"

"And GED? Please. If I needed it, Bentley could hack my way to a doctorate in rocket science, and I could forge the degree on the wall myself." Jo slumped back under the covers. "I'll take my chances in the real world, thanks."

I would have argued about her flawed logic and how our rooftop stakeouts, chop-shop takedowns and encounters with corrupt cops were infinitely more dangerous than the public education system, but my heart wasn't in it. All I could think about was the bridge.

"I don't know. The real world can be pretty overwhelming to some people."

"Are you saying you want to skip school and binge-watch Netflix? Because I am so up for that. What are you in the mood for? Funny? Scary?" She gave a knowing grin. "How about a police procedural, since you're dating a cop's son and all."

"Ha-ha, I'm so amused." I crossed my arms. I knew my next words would suck the funny right out of Jo. "I saw a girl this morning. She was about to jump off the Burrard Street Bridge."

Jo's face paled. She sat upright. "Are you serious?"

"Not something I'd joke about. I interrupted her, but she took off before I could get any closer." I rubbed at the knotted muscles in my neck, flinching when I skimmed my nape. My infinity tattoo had passed the scabbing phase, but the skin was still sensitive. The entire team had gotten the same ink in a show of solidarity and a "screw you" to those who'd thought they had control over us. We wouldn't be squashed down. The future was ours for the taking.

I felt more centered just thinking about the tattoo and what it stood for. What the team meant to me. The girl on the bridge probably could have used a symbol of hope like that. A few good people to stand by her.

"It's sticking with me, you know?" A quick glance at the microwave's glowing red numbers. "Got to shake it off. I have to hustle or I'll be late for first block."

"Raven, this is traumatic stuff. We should talk it out."

"Ah, no thanks." I didn't know why I'd said anything to Jo in the first place. I had to put the morning behind me.I shot a mournful look at my coffeemaker. No time for my morning fix. Diesel might have made sure I avoided my parents' fate, but caffeine was a true addiction.

I'd been drinking the stuff since before I'd hot-wired my first car.

"I'm going to grab a shower and head to school."

"Okaay." Jo drawled out the word.

I knew she wanted to keep digging at me, and I held my breath for the rush of questions that, thankfully, never came.

"Just don't use all the hot water," she said.

Big Daddy's hot-water tank was practically a tall bucket. The water would go from steaming to freezing in about four minutes, especially if I had the thing on full blast.

I let out an evil laugh.

"Ah, come on, Raven…"

FOUR

"I don't get it. What are we supposed to do?" Joel gnawed on the end of his pencil.

"Read the assignment," Brooke prompted. "Out loud this time."

Lucky me. I'd been teamed up with these two geniuses for a group history project.

Joel sighed. "Fine. It says, *Describe the steps that led to Canada achieving autonomy from Britain.* Then there's something about a line graph and a few dates we have to mention."

"What's *autonomy* again?"

Was I the only one who'd done the assigned reading? "*Autonomy*," I said. "Freedom. Independence. You know, how Canada became its own country?" Two sets of eyes blinked. Clueless. I choked back a groan. "I can see how this is going to go." I propped my feet, clad in faded black Doc Martens, on one of the empty chairs. "I'll do all the real work, and you guys will focus on coloring inside the lines."

"Nice! Why not tell us how you really feel?" Brooke seemed to give up at that point. She flopped back in her chair and proceeded to lose herself in her cell phone.

"We have to color?" Joel skimmed the assignment. "It doesn't say anything here about coloring."

Completely clueless. Before I could lose it on him, Brooke jabbed her cell in the air between us.

"You have to see this. A girl from our school just jumped off a bridge, and someone posted it online." She pressed

Play, squinting at the hazy footage. "Oh wow, that's Kendra Wallace. She's in my chemistry class."

Brooke enlarged the narrow image flickering across the screen. Whoever took the footage had made a quick pass along the bridge before focusing on the small form perched on the railing. My heart sank at the view of Burrard Street Bridge in the fog.

My eyes locked on the screen. Almost the exact scene I'd witnessed that morning, only this time there were a lot of people on the bridge trying to talk the girl down. Down she went all right. One second she was there. Wavering. Leaning forward. Then she was gone.

"No way." Joel gasped. "Now that's what I call autonomy. Freedom on your own terms, all the way. Play it again."

Really? How could they watch a girl do that to herself? And how could I have left, knowing what she'd tried to do earlier?

I should have waited around. Watched to see if she came back. This was Supersize all over again. The young apprentice I'd been training to climb. The kid who'd died because I hadn't been watching out for him like I should have.

Bile flooded the back of my mouth. I stood abruptly, knocking Brooke's cell from her hand. It clattered onto her desk.

"Hey…" she started to complain over the loud ringing of the school bell.

But I was already bolting for the door.

I squeezed into the hall that was crammed with bodies making their way to their next class. My cell pulsed in the back pocket of my skinny jeans.

Very few people had my number.

I moved closer to the lockers and out of the direct line of traffic. I checked my phone. A text. From Bentley.

WE GOT A LIVE ONE.

Not *Code Red*, since the team had declared hatred for the phrase when I used it, but someone must have reached out to us, needing our particular brand of assistance.

THE BAT CAVE. 9 PM.

It made my heart lighter to know Bentley could make me laugh out loud when, seconds before, I had been ready to heave up my guts. I fired him a quick response, telling him I'd be there with nunchucks on. Jo *had* called me a ninja. I tucked my cell back in my pocket and started toward the chem lab.

A sudden solid grip on my arm had me whirling in anger.

"Get off me, creeper, or I'll…" Um, yeah, what would I do? Words failed me. The buzzing activity of the hallway faded into the background as I stared up into the one face I couldn't stop thinking about.

"That's the best you can do? *Creeper*?" Laughter edged Emmett's voice. "You must have skipped your morning pot of coffee."

I groaned. "Don't remind me. I'm fighting off a killer withdrawal headache." I frowned. "How did you know I can't function without java in the morning?" Squinting in mock anger, I guessed, "Are you having me watched? Your dad got a man on me?"

Emmett scoffed. "I do my own investigating, thanks. No need to tap into police resources. I took a sip from the water bottle you always drag around. I know about the coffee." He avoided my gaze.

To my fascination, a flush worked up his jaw.

Only Emmett could blush at having to admit he'd swiped a drink without asking. Ever the law-abiding citizen.

"Only it wasn't water. Cold coffee tastes like...like..." He grimaced. "I don't know, it's just disgusting."

Laughing, I shook my head. "That's what you get for the grabby hands."

Emmett's gaze glittered with interest. Now it was my turn to blush.

"I'll take whatever I can get from you, Raven." He stared down at me from his substantial height advantage. "You know that."

I sucked in a breath. He certainly knew how to throw me off balance with a few smooth lines. Emmett had removed his hand from my arm the moment he got my attention, and I wanted to drag it back in place again. I liked it when he touched me. When we connected. Probably too much.

"But since you mentioned my dad…" Emmett shifted on his feet. "He asked about you. Wants you to come to the house." His eyes met mine. "He'll grill up some steaks. I can't promise the food will be any good, he usually burns everything, but come anyway."

This was unexpected. I retreated a step. "When?"

"Tonight."

Another strategic retreat. "I can't."

Emmett moved forward, closing in. "Why not?"

"I have a thing." I took a step to the left.

Emmett countered. "With Jo and the guys? Maybe I can help. I've helped before."

"I know, but it's no big deal." I had no idea if it was or wasn't, but I wanted to keep Emmett and the team as separate as possible. His dad meant well, but he was a cop. Sure, he'd been a solid resource in the past, but he couldn't be thrilled that his son had taken a shine to a girl who walked on the far side of the law. Plus Emmett was the one thing I had all to myself. He was pure. And clean. And good. I wanted him to stay that way.

"It's just a thing." Glancing around, I took in the empty hallway. "We're late for class." I deked around his tense body. "I have to go."

"Raven…"

"I can't, Emmett. I'm sorry."

"My dad won't stop." He didn't take my arm again—he didn't have to.

His low words had me frozen at his side. "He wants answers. I know I said I wouldn't push, that I'd wait until you were ready, but I worry about you. Every day." His voice hardened a little. "If you're such a risk taker, why not take a chance on me? Why can't you let me in?" Then he turned and walked away, without looking back.

He didn't get it.

I *could* let him in. All too easily.

That's what I was afraid of.

FIVE

At the back corner of the chem lab, I toiled over several beakers, feeling like a modern-day Victor Frankenstein—you know, without the reanimated corpse. Still, the setting was just about right. Rows of glass-door cabinets filled with ominous-looking jars and metal devices. Sterile workstations and double stainless-steel sinks. And twenty-two other mad scientists hard at work on their creations.

"All right, folks," Ms. Scott said from behind her own station at the front of the class, "let's get started. Remember to take a temperature reading with your thermometer every thirty seconds." She held up her hands. "And whatever you do, do *not* try to cool thermometers between uses. If you place a hot thermometer in cold water, it will crack, and I will not be happy."

A few students snickered. I fought a grin. The only thing that might crack was Scott's face if she tried to smile. I didn't think the woman was ever happy.

"Instead," she continued, "wipe them off with the paper towel I've provided." Scott glanced at her handheld timer. "And…go."

The entire class got to work.

I turned on the Bunsen burners and prepared to take notes on the different reaction times. The point of the experiment was to pinpoint the melting and freezing points of various liquids. Water. Vegetable oil. And an unknown sample that looked and smelled like urine. *Ugh.* I so hoped it wasn't, because then I wouldn't have to think about who or what kind of critter provided the goods.

The experiment reminded me of Team Retribution and how we were different, yet the same. We each had our own reaction times, some quicker to boil than others. There was hotheaded Jo, and then Jace, so cool and calculating. Bentley, always simmering but never out of control. But we all wanted the same thing—justice.

The sharp, unmistakable popping sound of shattering glass broke the intense silence and the zone I'd slipped into. *Uh-oh*. Someone hadn't listened to Scott.

Amateurs.

The sudden commotion from the middle of the room had the entire class and Ms. Scott staring in shock. What the…? Two guys faced off in the aisle between workstations. I recognized the taller one, Cody. And his friend Jonah. But I could barely process what I was seeing.

They both stood frozen in place. Jonah had his arms outstretched, reaching for Cody, though not in a violent way. This wasn't a middle-of-the-class throwdown. It was something else. Something way worse.

"Let me have that," Jonah pleaded, motioning for Cody to hand something over.

But what?

I peered through the bodies that had shifted into an instinctive spectator circle around the action. Slipped between a few kids. And then I saw it.

Cody held a broken thermometer in his hand, with the sharp, jagged edge pressed against his own throat. A bead of blood slipped down his neck, the stark red shocking against the white and chrome surrounding us.

"I need to," he mumbled. "I need it to stop. I can't live like this."

This couldn't be happening.

Not right in front of me.

Not again.

Skirting the wall of students, I approached Cody from behind and to the side. Jonah shot me a panicked look, shaking his head wildly to hold me off. It was enough of a distraction that Cody lowered the makeshift knife a few inches. He turned my way.

This was my only chance.

I held my breath and charged, knocking the thermometer out of his grip. As if released from a spell, the others jerked into action. A girl snatched up the weapon and handed it over to a shaken Ms. Scott, who was using her cell phone to call the office for assistance. Two boys now restrained Cody in a concerned but firm clasp.

Knowing Cody was contained and more help was on the way, I stepped back toward the exit. Several kids watched me go, probably freaked that I'd taken such a risk and wondering why I didn't stay to see what happened next.

But I'd had enough for one day.

SIX

"You're such a diva." Jace threw the words at a very animated Jo, who caught them from across the marble countertop of the island unit smack dab in the middle of Jace's oversized and rather industrial kitchen.

"And you're a Jackson Pollock gone bad," she replied with a decidedly unroyal sneer. Always with the art references.

Jace laughed. "Is that an insult? Because I'm sure any Pollock is worth a fortune."

"There's no accounting for taste."

A dark eyebrow rose. "You're trying to tell me you don't believe Pollock was one of the most innovative painters…"

And on they went, with Jo backpedaling because she was an artist herself and, of course, appreciated Pollock, but had talked herself into a corner.

Usually these two provided endless opportunities for amusement, but the craziness of the day was sticking in my gut. I wasn't in the mood for I-want-to-kiss-your-face-off-but-for-whatever-reason-I-won't banter.

It was cute. But under the circumstances? Unacceptable.

"Newb!" I glared at Jo. "Silver Spoon," I snarled at Jace. "Can we please just let Sir Bentley call this meeting of headcases to order?"

Bentley sat at the end of the island, hidden behind his laptop. As usual. At the mention of his name, he peered over the screen. "I like the *Sir*, Raven. That works for me. Everyone please use it in the future."

Jace's hand moved with swift precision as he smacked the back of his brother's head. "Careful, egghead. You sound an awful lot like—"

He stopped himself at the look on Bentley's face, but we all filled in the blanks.

The one thing that got Bentley's back up? Anything to do with Jace and Bentley's doctor father. And being compared to him? Not cool. Now *that* man was a bona fide mad scientist. He made good old Frankenstein seem like a preschooler forging mutants out of mismatched LEGO pieces.

Bentley hopped off his stool and stood to his full height. "You had to go there, didn't you?"

Jace held up a hand. "I'm sorry, that was out of line."

"Oh, a lame apology from Jace Almighty and everything's okay?" Bentley closed his laptop with the formality of a spaghetti-Western sharpshooter holstering his sidearm.

Jo and I exchanged a worried look. Jace was Bentley's older brother, his protector. They joked, they might get into heated debates, but they didn't outright fight. But we'd all been under increasing pressure now that more and more kids were contacting us and wanting our help taking down their own big bads. It was a responsibility we all felt compelled to meet, but the retribution gig wasn't without stressors.

Ripping each other new ones wasn't the solution. Sometimes it felt like this team of ours was hanging together by threads. Ever since we'd rescued Jo's friend Amanda from an undercover fight ring, we'd all been on edge. But we needed to get our act together. People out there were counting on us.

I slapped my hand on the cold marble. "Is there a full moon I don't know about? Would everybody please just chill and focus on the end game?"

"Raven's right," Jo said, hands on her hips. It didn't escape my notice that Jace was getting focused all right. On Jo's curves.

I rolled my eyes. *Guys.* They were so predictable.

"To answer your question, Raven," Bentley said from his perch back behind his laptop. Thankfully, he'd moved on and back to business. "According to NASA's online Sky Events Calendar, the next full moon will occur in seven days. There's also a blue moon, or two concurrent full moons in one lunar cycle, set to appear next month."

Bentley's timing, innocently pretending to answer my clearly rhetorical question, was perfect. It was hard to resist the smile pulling at my lips.

"Thank you, Bent." I noticed Jo and Jace fighting grins as well.

"Anytime. Now, if you could all take your seats. I've got a few potential cases, but one is time sensitive, and I suggest we start there."

Weird how we'd gone from one random kid contacting Bentley, and us agreeing to work as a team, to these meetings. Here was where we evaluated and deliberated and then selected which cry for help seemed the most desperate. The most worthy.

And, frankly, the most fun.

Sometimes revenge really was sweet.

SEVEN

And sometimes revenge was just plain boring. *Ugh*. Stakeouts were the worst. I'd taken what I thought was going to be a case I could sink my teeth into, yet here I was, only a few days in and chomping at the bit for some real action.

According to Bentley, Jonathan McNair's brand-new stepmother, who was only a few years older than his own sixteen years of age, was trying to kill him. She was doing this, Jonathan claimed, so she could inherit all of his middle-class, working-stiff father's fortune.

Which, Bentley admitted, was pretty measly. The guy worked at a recycling plant.

Still, Jonathan was convinced stepmommy dearest was poisoning his food. She'd made no secret of her disregard for his love of video games and cosplay. Said he'd never get a girlfriend that way, and she wasn't going to let him live in their basement until he was thirty-five. He knew she wanted him out of the way as soon as possible.

Then he'd started to feel off. He'd been getting worse every day since she'd suddenly developed a fixation with bulking him up. According to our guy, this was a ploy to get him and his father out of the kitchen while she prepared complex meals.

Gone were the days of his father's super-garlicky, super-spicy, super-good spaghetti and meatballs. Now Jonathan could hardly pronounce the ingredients his stepmother used in her dishes.

Jace, our resident boxer and fitness guru, was familiar with a strict diet, but even he scarfed down a greasy hamburger now and then. He'd had no interest in taking on this case, and Jo was recovering from her last one.

So here I was, parked across the street from Jonathan's place, my wheels for the evening a black Mazda3 Sport—not flashy enough to get noticed on the streets of this neighborhood, but with the guts to make the risk worthwhile.

Once a car thief, always a car thief.

Besides, I would return it to the parkade as soon as I was done. I didn't steal for keepsies anymore—just borrowed here and there.

I jogged across the street, careful to keep to the shadows, and slunk around to the side entrance. Jonathan had promised to leave the door unlocked that night. They'd gone to the movies, a tradition started by his real mother that he had insisted his father uphold.

The handle turned easily. I was kind of disappointed. I needed to keep my lock-picking skills at their prime.

My phone buzzed in my pocket. Bentley, checking in.

"Yo." I spoke as I made my way to the kitchen.

"Yo back," Bentley said. "Jonathan has texted me a thousand times wondering if you've found anything yet. Are you in?"

"Yeah." I began opening cupboards, looking for a bag of pills or vial of some toxic liquid. "I've got a ton of Tupperware without lids, your basic canned goods and the normal spices."

A pop-down TV was mounted under one of the cupboards. For kicks, I turned it on. The laugh track from a sitcom echoed through the room.

"Is someone there?" Panic laced Bentley's voice.

"Nope, just put the boob tube on for a little mood setting."

"You're odd."

"Why, thank you." I opened the pantry. Blinked in awe at the amount of product I saw on the middle shelf. "Bent, text Jonny boy. Ask him what kind of symptoms he's been having."

"You found something?"

"Just do it." I ended the call, confident I'd cracked the case. Thank god they weren't all this easy or I'd be out of the retribution gig in a heartbeat.

This wasn't even challenging. Another gut-bursting round of laughter from the TV. I couldn't get sympathy anywhere.

My phone pulsed.

"His guts have been in knots," Bentley said in my ear. "Anything he eats comes out as liquid. Number one and number two."

Ugh. Not a great visual.

"She's not trying to kill him." I sighed. "She's on a health kick. Looks like she's been adding bran to everything. There's enough here to unblock a *T. rex* after an all-you-can-eat Triceratops buffet."

Bentley laughed. "I'm thinking you went through a dinosaur phase when you were a kid. I'm right, aren't I?"

He was, but I'd never admit it. Our resident hacker already had too much potential blackmail material on me. "Tell Jonathan we're done. He can handle it from here."

"It's a crappy job—" Bentley began.

"But somebody's got to do it." I finished with a laugh of my own.

Then the laughter died in my throat as a montage clip on the screen drew my eyes to the mini TV. Photos of a young girl. And a guy about my age. I moved closer. He looked familiar. The haggard faces of two tearful parents filled the screen. What were they saying? A murder-suicide?

The reporter began filling in the details. "In a tragic series of events, fifteen-year-old Cody Fisher ended his life after taking that of his twelve-year-old sister Emma. The parents discovered their children upon arriving home from work…"

I should have stayed. I should have made sure Cody was okay. That they'd followed up properly. This was on me. All the way.

"Raven? You still there?"

"Bentley," I choked out. "I need you to do me a favor. Please." He must have heard the desperation in my voice.

"Anything."

EIGHT

By the time I pulled up in front of the East Hastings Community Kitchen to pick up Jo, Bentley had hacked into my school's server and accessed the records on Kendra and Cody. It was just too weird that two kids from my school had killed themselves in the same week.

"Both of them had been sent to the school counselor, Mrs. Chappet, for help dealing with test-anxiety issues," Bentley informed us during a conference-call update. "Unfortunately, the electronic trail ends there. I haven't been able to scare up any other details online, but I'll keep digging."

Jace was on the line too. "If Chappet is old school, there might be handwritten files with more information in her office somewhere."

It was as good a lead as any.

"Jo and I will look into it," I said as Jo approached the car. She opened the Mazda's passenger door and climbed inside.

"You *borrowing* this one too?" She glanced around the hatchback's slick interior.

"I'll have it back by morning. Pinky swear."

We peeled away from the curb.

Jo volunteered plenty of hours at the kitchen in exchange for groceries. The guy who ran the place, Clem, was ex-military and looked out for Jo and other teens who just needed someone to give them a break. Recently, while we were helping Jo find Amanda, we'd learned there was a lot more to Clem than we'd thought. A good thing—we needed everyone we could get.

"Thanks for this," I said, keeping my eyes on the road.

"My pleasure." Jo lowered the passenger window and wove her hand through the rush of air. "We both know you need me to watch your back."

"Riiighhht," I drawled. That wasn't why I was dragging her along. I might not need her assistance to get inside my school and do some digging around in filing cabinets. But if I was being honest with myself, my head was seriously messed up—I wanted Jo around to keep me in the here and now.

I was wrecked after not once but twice failing to help kids who deeply needed it. When Supersize died, I'd promised myself I would do whatever I could, whatever it took, to not feel like that again. And yet here I was, the same raw mixture of guilt, regret and rage making pretzels of my insides. At least Jo would have keen spidey senses if anything out of the ordinary happened on our recon mission.

After making short work of the teacher-access lock and the deadbolt on Chappet's door, we settled into rooting through a few five-drawer filing cabinets.

The counselor was a true hoarder. There were articles from various medical and psychiatric magazines dating all the way back to the '80s.

Zero files regarding students. I found myself growling in frustration as I opened yet another drawer of folders filled with clippings. "Argh...still nothing. It's like she's deliberately messing with us."

Jo groaned. "I know, right? Wait, what's this?" She pointed to an empty space among all the paper stacks and clutter on Chappet's desk, one about the size of a laptop. "I guess she's not so old school after all. She's probably got the student files on her laptop and takes it home every night. You'll have to wait until tomorrow and sneak back in here."

I bit back a curse and slammed the filing-cabinet drawer shut. The force jarred a few items off the top.

A sticky note fluttered to the floor at my feet.

Harborview Anxiety Treatment Center
Student referrals only.

Then two names, underlined.

Kendra
Cody

"Gotcha." I turned the note over in my hands. "Both of them were referred to this place. Both dead in the same week. I have to go and check it out."

Jo waved a few pages under my nose. "And I just found their referral letters— handwritten, as Jace predicted." She moved to the small photocopier in the corner of the office. "I can forge the shrink's handwriting and create a letter for you." Her grin was evil. "I knew that OCD of yours would come in handy someday."

I frowned. "What do you mean?"

"Your neat-freak impulses, the minor case of obsessive-compulsive disorder you're sporting. OCD is all part of anxiety, Raven." She smiled. "Unless you end up dead, this just might be good for you."

NINE

The Harborview Anxiety Treatment Center was located close enough to the business district to have a sheen of clout, but still on the fringe of things, so rent would be decent. Several businessman types exited the Italian restaurant across the street. Among them I spied a familiar face. One of the suits was somebody Diesel used to meet with at the chop shop. Yeah, the area was definitely surface kosher with a side of sketchy.

I covered my hair with my hoodie and kept my head low as I approached the center's double-door entrance. A woman pushed through the doors, almost taking me out. She was hissing into her phone. I caught a bit of the conversation "...I just left. I told her I can't be a part of it anymore..."

Hmm...Someone didn't seem too happy. I grabbed the handle and pulled, scanning the street with a quick look over my shoulder. The suits weren't paying the woman or me, any attention. Good while Diesel was safely behind bars, his cronies weren't. It wasn't like I'd gone into hiding after his chop shop had been abandoned and later dismantled by the cops. No one from my former life of crime had sought me out. But I wasn't taking any chances.

I stepped inside.

Classical music piped through the empty reception area. For anyone else, the hushed cellos and violins probably created an instant feeling of calmness, which made sense in this kind of place.

But the droning strings just grated on my nerves. Now a grungy classic-rock tune? That could lull me to sleep anytime.

"Welcome to Harborview. May I help you?"

I spun around. A woman was now standing behind the counter, her arms crossed, her gaze hard.

"Sure, yeah..." I stammered, not even faking my unease. Heights didn't bother me a smidge, but the thought of a medical professional digging at me for insights into my character had me quaking in my Docs. "My name's Raven. The school counselor sent me." I handed her the referral letter Jo had whipped up.

The woman stared at me for another long, uncomfortable moment, and then her eyes darted to the letter. "Ah, you're from Laurier Secondary. Mrs. Chappet has sent several other students our way lately. I'm happy to report we've been the key factor in eliminating their suffering."

I choked back a snort. That was one way to spin the facts. Oh, I so wanted to get the dirt on these medical monsters.

"I'm so pleased to meet you, Raven. I'm Dr. Millie," the woman continued. She glanced around the reception area. "I hope you weren't waiting long. Our receptionist has stepped out for lunch."

I bit back a laugh. Is that what you're calling it when staff quits on you? Stepping out for lunch?

"Now, if you'll follow me," Dr. Millie said over her shoulder as she led the way down the hall, "we can chat in one of our meeting rooms."

I followed her into a tiny office consisting of a table, several chairs and a noticeable lack of windows. The walls were painted a deep mustard yellow, which was probably supposed to reflect sunshine and happiness. To me it looked like the inside of a submarine.

Dr. Millie started to close the door behind us, but I blocked the slab with my foot. "Do you mind?" I gave a sheepish shrug. "I'm not so good with small spaces." Jo had said to throw down any and all anxiety issues I could think of. Claustrophobia seemed like a no-brainer in a place like this.

"Whatever you need, Raven. Quite a common request from our clients, I assure you."

Even though I was faking it, deliberately choosing a basic fear experienced by a ton of people, I still hated Millie's smug smile. Three minutes into my infiltration and I wanted to bail. Not a good sign. But there was more than my pride at stake. Kids were dying, and the fine, educated folk at this center were likely responsible.

I just had to prove it.

Millie sat down behind the desk, two water bottles in her hands. She offered me one.

"Water? Oh, no thanks." I waved a hand. "I'm trying to cut back." The doctor didn't so much as blink at my joke. "I'd kill for a cup of coffee though."

"We don't have sodas here, or coffee. You should know that caffeine can exacerbate anxiety symptoms. And you should definitely avoid any type of energy drink."

I'd never been a fan of energy drinks and ignored the inadvertent dig at my drug of choice. "In that case, sure, lay one on me." I twisted the lid and took a long swig of the lukewarm water, wishing it was a mug full of the finest, darkest roast at my favorite café. I dropped into the other chair.

"I can sense you're unsure," Millie said, setting her water aside and studying me carefully. "Being nervous is a completely rational response. You're taking a huge step toward your recovery. Remember, we're here as a resource for you, to help you get better. Knowing your triggers will go a long way."

"So what do we do now? Talk? About my feelings?" Again, I wasn't faking the tremor in my voice. I hated touchy-feely sharing and caring. "Or do you want to know my every random weird thought, like how I'm wondering if the walls in here are yellow for a reason? And you mentioned triggers. What do you do if the color yellow is a trigger for someone?" Thankfully, the doctor didn't seem interested in my awkward babble, just paperwork.

"If you would please take a moment to fill out this form, that would be great." The doctor slid a piece of paper and a pen across the desk. "Don't worry, it's nothing in-depth at this point," she added as I began reading and scratching in a few one-word responses. "We're interested in your medical history, any known allergies…and are you currently on any medication? Anti-depressants? Anything for your anxiety?"

I shook my head, casually feeding the doctor the backstory Jo and I had created. "My parents are a fan of the 'let's try exercise and a change of diet and see if that helps' approach. But Counselor Chappet convinced them, and me, that this was worth a shot."

"Wonderful. Having little previous exposure to other medications makes you an especially good candidate for our treatments. AL28-9, or ALLY, as we affectionately call it, because it *will* be your ally in defeating your anxiety, has been successful for 97 percent of our drug-trial participants."

Ah, so it was a drug trial, and obviously floating under the radar. Too bad the kids who'd signed up had had the misfortune to trust the adults around them. Like our school counselor, who was supposed to be looking out for them, not peddling a cure-all that hadn't been fully investigated.

."Those are very good odds for you."
Millie's eyes narrowed. "And your parents
couldn't make it today?"

"Nope." I shrugged. Fielding questions
about my parents was another no-brainer.
I'd been doing it for years. "Mom said it
was time I took some responsibility for
myself and my issues. She was just glad
the counselor knew of this option for kids
like me."

"That's fine. We do have a consent form
for them to sign, but for now your signature
will do." Millie whisked that form away
the moment I'd scrawled my signature at
the bottom. I'd barely had time to read the
heading, *Authorization for Medical Treatment.*

I watched as the doctor made a show of
putting my newly created file, containing
the forms I'd just filled out, into a drawer.

The doctor's satisfied smile was chilling.
"There. Now you're officially one of ours."

TEN

"She called it ALLY but let the real name slip—AL28-9."

"Got it. I'll see what I can find in the usual medical journals and various other sources that might actually offer me a challenge." Bentley's fingers flew over his keyboard. "You know…" His tone switched from confident hacker to pestering pester. "This could be a good thing. There's nothing quite like bonding over a family barbecue."

Ugh. I never should have told him about Emmett's invite. And why was everyone suddenly so worried about what was good for me? This was one of the problems with getting close to people— they felt entitled to have opinions about how you ran your life. Well, that worked both ways. "I'm sure there were plenty of greasy burgers grilled at your place," I said. "Your parents really seem the type."

Bentley snorted. "Mother would have fainted at the carbs in the buns alone." He shot me a sideways glance, fingers still tapping out code. "All right, so I have no idea what occurs at such events. But look at it this way—your thing with Emmett aside, his dad is an asset we need to retain. We take out the trash and then he puts it away, making the streets of our fair city that much safer."

"That's not the problem." I groaned. He'd hit the nail on the head of the other major issue I had with letting people in. "The more I get to know Emmett, the worse I feel about all the lying—to him and his dad. I'm using him. Them. We are. And I hate it."

Bentley spun in his chair. "Now wait a minute. This arrangement we have isn't all one-sided. Emmett's dad is getting noticed in the force. I've been monitoring his emails and—"

I gripped one arm of his swivel chair and spun him hard.

It took a few seconds before Bentley could touch the floor with his feet and stop his momentum. "Not nice, Raven."

"And spying on someone who's trying to help us is?"

"It's called due diligence. You think Jo's going to blindly trust a cop after what one did to her family? Or that Jace would walk into any situation without covering all the bases?"

I bit my lip. Bentley was right. That Jo had allowed Emmett and his dad in as much as she had was pretty much a miracle, considering all she'd been through. And Jace was the ultimate strategist, not willing to move a pawn on the board without working through every contingency.

"You know about our parents, Jo's and all she lost…" Bentley paused. "But you never talk about yours."

"My losses?"

"Your parents, Raven. Unless you were dropped into that chop shop by a car-thieving, egg-laying stork?"

I swallowed back a lump of emotion. "There's not much to tell. It's the usual story. My folks were addicts, they left me to fend for myself, and then Diesel offered me a way off the streets."

"Hmm…"

"Don't hmm me, Bent. I'm not in the mood."

"There's got to be more. How old were you when Diesel found you? Where were you living?"

"Well, I wasn't hanging out in the Wayne Manor, that's for sure. What's with all the questions? Why do you even care?"

I regretted my harsh words the moment I spoke them, but I'd been on edge for days. Bentley's prodding was the last straw. Things I hadn't told anyone else began spewing out of my mouth.

"I was about six, okay? Just a stupid little kid. I had to feed myself, dress myself and, most of all, I had to keep myself safe. From them. When Diesel took me in, he was like a god to me. I never looked back. But he knew, somehow, that I'd always wonder. He kept tabs on them for me in case I ever asked about them. Which I did, a few times. But a year ago he told me his leads had dried up. He tried to locate them but couldn't. Suspected they'd finally gone too far. OD'd. But now I don't know—was he telling the truth? Or was everything he said and did a lie right from the very beginning?"

Bentley was quiet for a long time. Then he stunned me with an offer that had my stomach dropping to the floor. "I could find them for you."

I held a hand to my churning guts. "Don't, don't you dare, Bent. I mean it." I bolted for the door. "Leave it alone. I don't look back. Ever. I can't."

But it was too late. He'd reached deep into my heart and sliced open a wound I'd thought had scarred over long ago.

ELEVEN

Fireflies flickered in the shrubs along the fence enclosing Emmett's yard in a mix of weathered wood and overgrown greenery. The cozy glow did nothing to put me at ease. In fact, the almost fantastical setting had me clenching my teeth until my jaw ached. This was worse than the classical music at the treatment center.

"Another soda, Raven?" Officer Daniels—I just couldn't think of him as Emmett's dad—reached into a cooler and tossed a can my way even though I hadn't replied.

I caught the can an inch from my nose. Wow. Throwing projectiles at his son's dinner date sent quite the message. Next time it could be a bullet. Probably not, but still…I studied the wrinkles around his eyes. They could be from laughing. They could be from something much worse.

Like him plotting my downfall.

Emmett watched from across the patio dining table, a smirk on his face. He was loving this.

I aimed for his shin, but only managed to kick a table leg. Pain shot through my foot. My muffled curse had Emmett laughing out loud.

Officer Daniels stopped chewing. "Did she just kick you?"

"She tried."

"You're right—she does have endearing qualities."

Endearing qualities? Just what else had Emmett told his father about me? I squirmed in my seat, not comfortable with the idea of them talking about me when I wasn't around to defend myself. Besides, I wasn't endearing. I was a major badass.

I chomped into my hamburger without mercy. Maybe that was the appeal for Emmett. A way for him to get under his father's skin. The cop's son hooking up with a bad girl from the wrong side of the tracks. If we had any train tracks in this town.

Maybe Emmett was using me as much as I was using him.

I decided I was fine with that. In fact, it actually helped us make sense.

So why did the burger suddenly taste like secondhand vomit in my mouth?

"Raven..." Officer Daniels's light-hearted tone darkened. "You know why I asked Emmett to bring you here."

Looked like the gloves were coming off. Finally. "You want information about Team Retribution."

He tilted his head. "Is that what you're calling yourselves?"

"On good days. Mostly I call the others ginormous pains in my butt." I shoved my plate aside. "There's not much to tell. You already get the gist of what we do, what we are."

"But not who you are. I need to know more about your team, Raven. There's you, another girl Emmett has met once, but the rest…"

"Are just a couple of guys with similar interests."

"And those interests would be in stolen vehicles, forgeries, obtaining highly classified information and essentially blackmailing criminals?"

"Dad—" Emmett started, holding up his hand as if to block his father's words from reaching me.

I stopped him mid-breath with a light touch to his wrist. "Not to mention taking down corrupt police officers," I said pointedly. "I appreciate the wining and dining, Officer Daniels, but if this is a setup, let's get on with it." I glanced around the dreamlike yard, pulse pounding, willing myself to remain calm. "Are your boys hiding in the shrubbery? Should I start packing for juvie?"

A zing of tension had my muscles clenching. My jaw locked.

Emmett swore under his breath. "Raven, you've got this all wrong. He just wants to know who he's working with."

"Emmett's right." Officer Daniels interlaced his fingers. "I've put my career in jeopardy by helping you. There's interest in your team. Questions from my superiors."

I pulled in a deep breath. "But you haven't told them anything."

"I wouldn't have much to say, would I? I've met you. Emmett has had contact with your friend Jo. But we don't know the other members of your team." He studied me with serious eyes. "The thefts, the breaking and entering—those alone weren't enough to put you on the radar, but you kids have been slicing through high-level, tightly secured resources like their firewalls are made of mosquito netting. That doesn't go unnoticed. If things ever go south, give me the name of your hacker and I know I can get the rest of you total immunity."

My stomach dropped at the thought of betraying Bentley and Jace that way. "Not going to happen."

He lifted his hands in surrender. "Purely worst-case scenario."

Speaking of worst cases, my cell phone hummed from my jeans pocket. Just as I glanced at the screen, Officer Daniels got a text as well. We stared at our screens. My message was from Jace. The body of another teen had been found, this time in my school gym.

"I have to go," we said simultaneously to Emmett.

He frowned back at us, his shoulders stiff with tension. "Now? Both of you?"

"It's not like we were having the time of our lives anyway." I stood, ignoring Officer Daniels's irritated sideways glance. "I'll see you at school." I paused. "If there is school tomorrow. I guess it depends."

"What does that mean?" Emmett's puzzled expression had nothing on his father's angry one. "What's going on at the school?"

"Your source sure is fast, Raven," Officer Daniels said. "But I do not want to see a hint of you at the scene. Not even your shadow. Are we clear? Because if I do—"

But he was ranting at dead air. I'd already slipped across the yard, away from the warm lights and deeper into the darkness.

"Raven, wait." Emmett jogged after me.

"My ride's this way." Vaulting forward, I quickly scrambled up the fence. I swung my legs over the top, ready to drop into the alley behind the Daniels property.

"Would you just hold on?" Emmett's voice was thick with frustration and disappointment.

I met his gaze, conscious of the deep rumble of Jace's car growing louder with every breath.

"I didn't think Dad would get into things tonight." Emmett rested his palms on the fence boards.

"It's okay."

"I wanted you to have fun. For him to see how great you are. Don't let this be an excuse to not see me again."

I let out a sigh. Now was the time to say something deep and meaningful. To tell him I understood, that tonight and his father's not-so-subtle threats didn't matter. That I still liked him anyway. But the words were having a boxing match behind my teeth.

A squeal of tires echoed in the night. Speaking of boxing…

"Let's go," Jace called from his car. "We have to hurry."

I shoved away from the fence and landed hard for such a short distance, my mind and body out of sync. I charged for the vehicle.

Slamming the passenger door shut, I let Jace speed us far from the hurt in Emmett's eyes.

There wasn't a vehicle in the world that could drive fast enough.

TWELVE

Breaking into a school at night was usually a no-brainer, but breaking into a school that was now a designated crime scene, complete with several police cruisers and freaked-out neighbors, was a little more tricky.

Unless you could climb the building and get a bird's-eye view.

I shimmied farther along the rafters high above the polished gym floor. Jace had dropped me off near the side entrance, and I'd taken my usual route up the exterior wall to the rooftop entrance. It was easy enough to open the small metal hatch and drop down into one of the custodial rooms. I landed lightly on my feet, narrowly avoiding a mop bucket full of murky water.

I cracked open the industrial door and took a quick look down the hall. Then sucked in a breath and sealed it shut again as a police officer strode by. I waited until the tread of his footsteps faded, then tried once more. The coast was clear. I cut across the hall to another door and slipped inside. I followed the narrow staircase that wound backstage to the second-story access point. The landing was about four feet wide and stuffed with additional props, costumes and backdrops.

I shoved a mangled Christmas tree out of my path and climbed the railing. I jumped up and reached for the metal beam overhead. Time to straddle the rafters.

"Can you hear me now? Raven? Planet Earth to Operation Big Bird. Where is she?" Bentley's voice came through loud and clear in my earpiece, startling me. I bit back a curse and adjusted my grip. "I told you we should have tested the two-way communication link before using it live in the field."

In the field. Bentley did love his spy talk. I snorted.

"Hey, I think I've got her. Raven, are you in?"

"What do you think?" I whispered roughly. "Now will you pipe down?" From my vantage point I could easily observe the investigation below.

Several police and ambulance crew members had gathered by the bleachers, blocking my view as they filled Officer Daniels in on the situation. We'd arrived at almost the same time. As they talked, Daniels scanned the gym with keen eyes. He was clearly on the lookout for me.

Adrenaline flared, and I took in a few slow, steady breaths. I had to remain completely still. One wrong move and the rafters would creak and reveal my hiding place.

Police officers buzzed around the gym, taping off the area and photographing the scene. Occasionally shoulders shifted and I caught sight of denim-clad legs and cross-trainers. *Ugh*. Not a sight you ever wanted to see. A guy's body dangled from the highest peak under the bleachers.

His face. For a second I swore his mouth was opening and closing, desperate for air. It was all in my head. It had to be.

I turned away, forcing down the bile that surged up my throat. I kept my gaze fixed on the wooden rafters as the EMTs and police cut the body down. Once it was covered and wheeled out of the gym, the officers' voices grew in volume and echoed across the gym, bouncing off the cinder-block walls.

"The evening custodian found the boy around 7:40 PM." A cop was briefing Daniels. "He immediately called 9-1-1, then followed up with the principal and informed her of what he'd discovered."

"And the note?" asked Officer Daniels.

The cop nodded. "Bagged it." He handed Daniels a plastic bag containing a piece of paper.

Daniels held it delicately, reading aloud. "*I never meant to let you down, Dad.*"

My stomach twisted at hearing the last words of this boy being read while his body was being photographed a few feet away.

"*I'm sorry I failed you. I failed the team. I tried, but it wasn't enough. I'll never be enough.*" Clearing his throat, Daniels returned the evidence. "The note is addressed to his father. He doesn't mention anyone else."

"No. The mother died a few years ago. Cancer. My son used to play on the basketball team as well, before he blew his knee out. Anyway, I remember her coming to the games, right to the end." He cleared his throat. "Ryan was their only child."

Daniels shook his head. "Horrible thing, suicide."

My jaw clenched.

If what we suspected was true…

It was horrible, all right, but it wasn't suicide.

It was murder.

THIRTEEN

"So what are you saying?" Jo hopped up to sit on the marble countertop. "We don't help kids anymore?" She swiped an apple from a glass bowl and took a bite with an angry crunch.

Jace leaned a shoulder against the ginormous stainless-steel fridge, while Bentley sat on a barstool, ignoring the rest of us and tapping away on his laptop.

"Nooo." I dragged the one-syllable word out for all it was worth. "But the McNair case was a joke. If I'd been following up on the Cody situation instead of dealing with that total waste of our time, maybe we could have done something. I might have gotten to him before he…" I struggled with the thought of Cody taking his own life. Add to that his little sister's, and I could barely think at all. "And the other guy, Ryan—I can't get the image of his body swaying in the air out of my mind."

"Raven." Jace shook his head. "You can't blame yourself. Or us. We're just skimming the surface of what's going on here. But I do hear what you're saying about weeding through the sob stories and only taking on the most important jobs. I'm sure Jo understands where you're coming from too."

Jo shrugged. "No more small beans. I can live with that." She pointed her half-eaten apple at me. "But how do you propose we decide which is which? Eenie, meenie, miney, mo? Not a super-efficient system."

I opened my mouth to say we'd pretty much been doing exactly that, but Bentley spoke first.

"I'll do more research, background searches, dig a bit more before bringing you guys the potentials." He tapped his screen like it held all the answers. "I probably should have done that before we agreed to help Jonathan anyway. If you need someone to blame, Raven, blame me."

Bentley was the last person who should have felt bad about the current situation. He'd constantly gone above and beyond for the team and had mad computer skills none of us could touch.

"It wasn't your fault, Bent," I said in a huff.

He shot me a sad grin. "Wasn't yours either."

Jace clapped his hands together, making us jump. "Right, Bentley will establish some sort of evaluation protocol, and we'll go from there. It's obvious this is top of the list, so let's focus, shall we? Raven, what do you have?"

"The guy, Ryan, was sixteen and captain of the senior boys' basketball team," I said. "I talked to a few kids, and the general consensus was that he was a decent guy, good student, liked to party but wasn't a dick about it, and he lived for sports. College scouts have been sniffing around, and it seemed like the world was his for the taking. The guys on the team said he was getting pressure from his dad to up his game to secure the best scholarship possible."

Jace nodded. "Pressure like that can mess with your head."

Jo tossed her apple core into the shiny silver garbage can. "Enough for a visit to the school counselor?"

"Maybe." I bit my lip, frustrated. "There's got to be a way to stop this."

"We have to," Jace said sternly. He glanced at his brother. "We know what it's like to have someone play Frankenstein with your life."

Bentley's eyes hardened. "What our father did was wrong. And so is this. But he wasn't invincible, and neither are these jerks."

I was glad to see the brothers working together again.

"Here's what I've collected so far." Bentley spun his laptop to face us and clicked through a bunch of websites and saved documents. "The pharmaceutical industry and the minds behind it have been conducting illegal drug trials since the early 1900s. They've always found ways to rush their product through the system. Legally, trial subjects must give what they call *informed consent*. They're supposed to sign a contract that outlines potential risks, but all of those details are also supposed to be explained verbally too so there's no confusion. And pharmaceutical companies need to outline the study in full and obtain permission beforehand from organizations like Health Canada or the Federal Drug Administration. In addition to all of that, minors need parental consent to participate, and trials usually follow a set pattern. Testing begins with animals, then human adults and finally children. They're super cautious about anything involving kids."

"So when I get inside—"

"When you *infiltrate* the facility…"

I smiled. Bent and his spy talk again. "Right. When I infiltrate this thing, they should be asking me for a referral from a medical doctor and insisting on getting my parents to sign forms, and they should have a sit-down to explain the details."

"If they're legit, sure. All of that and probably more. But I can't find any indication that a trial is currently underway, either on animals or humans. Which means if they're running one, it's off the books. And another thing.

I did some digging, and the doctor in charge of the study recently presented a session on teen anxiety at an educators' conference. I'm betting your school isn't the only one sending kids her way."

"What's her name?"

"Dr. Serena Millie."

Figured. It was the same doctor who'd done the entrance interview with me. I'd officially met the head of the snake. Now it was time to cut it off.

"Let's get this show on the road."

FOURTEEN

"And Raven makes our sixth participant."
Dr. Millie waved me into the room.
"Everyone, meet Raven." A circle of faces
stared back at me. "Raven, this is Katie,
Moira, Vince, Cameron and Joel. There
will be plenty of time to get acquainted
once the trial officially begins. But first,
there are a few housekeeping issues we
need to take care of." She hitched her hip
onto the corner of her desk and crossed
her arms. "Thank you all for submitting
to our various physical-requirement
tests. The tongue swabs can tell us so

much about your general health. Did you know pale gums are a sign of immune deficiencies or anemia?"

Oh, she was full of fun facts. When none of us reacted with awe at her revelations, she continued, "Each of you is here of your own volition, with your own challenges you need to overcome. We're going to do everything within our power to help you succeed..."

I tuned out her very prepared speech, speculating on how many other kids must have heard the same thing. Stood right where I was standing, only to end up inside a body bag.

My phone buzzed. Shifting my body slightly, I checked out the text. Bentley, again.

Are you still in contact with Dr. Millie?

I sent a thumbs-up.

We think her daughter goes to our school.

That figured. Jace and Bentley attended the most elite private school in the city.

That the lead doctor working for a major pharmaceutical company sent her kid there wasn't a stretch.

Jace and Jo have a plan.

And that would be...?

I waited for a reply, but the doctor was watching me. I turned my phone off and stuffed it in my pocket.

Millie was still in full monologue mode. "...and all we ask is that you don't fight the process."

As if on cue, a man stepped into the doorway. His shoulders filled the frame. His smile held more than its share of bite. "Their bags have been loaded. The transport is ready when you are, Dr. Millie."

"Thanks, Simon. I'll send them along momentarily."

Transport? My pulse quickened. Damn, I should have realized...they were taking us off-site.

One of the girls held up a hand.

Millie smiled kindly. "Yes, Katie?"

"We're not staying here?"

"Not unless you want to sleep on the floor." The doctor laughed. "I'm sure we went over accommodations in our initial meetings." She ignored the confused glances we were all shooting each other. "Our office isn't equipped for overnight stays. Trust me, you'll be much more comfortable at the house. It's more of a small hotel, really. You'll have your own rooms, TVs, and we've even upgraded our video-game consoles. The latest and greatest. While you won't have Internet access, you won't be sentenced to a technology-free wasteland." She laughed again, sharing a patronizing look with the muscle guy, Simon. "We know how important tech is to you young people."

Millie opened the closest desk drawer. "That said, we do require your full attention and focus during the trial. Cell phones, please." Her smile was sickeningly sweet. "I promise they will be returned to you on Monday morning before checkout."

Under Simon's watchful gaze we took turns dropping our phones into the drawer. I kept my expression carefully blank as I let mine fall, thankful Bentley had installed heavy-duty encryption. Even if they cracked my password and skimmed through my messages, they wouldn't be able to decode my texts.

I wasn't worried about being incommunicado. Jo had insisted I take a backup burner, and I hadn't argued. We were both used to taking care of ourselves, and as much as I knew Jace and Bentley had our backs, neither of us trusted Team Retribution 100 percent. The burner was tucked inside the backpack that I'd taken for the two nights I'd be away. It was stuffed inside my rolled-up socks along with a change of clothes, a bottle of two-in-one shampoo-conditioner and my toothbrush.

The doctor kept droning on. "Don't think for a second we don't understand how difficult it can be to surrender yourself to the unknown. Each and every one of you is so very brave in taking this step." In a dramatic move, she placed a hand over her heart. "This is the day your lives change for the better." She gestured to the hallway. "Now how about we get started?"

We followed Simon to the back exit, where a twelve-passenger bus was waiting, engine running. Simon had stacked our bags on the last few seats, and we climbed in and sat at the front.

The bus pulled away from the curb. Keen to see where they were taking us, I cranked my head left and right.

But the windows had been completely blacked out with spray paint.

FIFTEEN

It was dark when the bus finally came to a stop. Simon guided us off, handing us our bags as we exited. A cold wind kicked dust around our feet. We stood in a shivering line, taking in what Millie called "the house."

If Millie was selling it as some sort of mini-resort, where was she used to laying her head? The Bates Motel?

The house was tall, dark and dingy, something out of a Hitchcock film.

I didn't have much time to take in our surroundings other than to establish we'd been brought to an older section of the city. I had tried to memorize the journey, but after ten minutes of twisting and turning, I could no longer tell if we were going north or south, east or west. Bentley would not be impressed.

* * *

I guessed this wasn't so bad. Even the food was above the usual hospital fare. Dinner was boxes of takeout pizza, spread out over the folding cafeteria-style tables in the converted office space they called the dining hall. It wasn't exactly a healthy offering, but it sure beat bland chicken and plastic containers filled with stale butterscotch pudding.

That was pretty much all I remembered from my one and only hospital stay, back when I'd first started climbing and botched an attempt to scale my first three-story building. I'd fallen hard and ended up with a broken collarbone. Diesel had made quick work of getting me out of the hospital. If he hadn't, I'd have ended up in the foster care system for sure. He'd been pleased to know I'd made a speedy recovery, even splurged and bought me some fast food on the way to the warehouse. I'd never been so happy to eat greasy burgers and fries.

"So what's your deal?" a guy asked me through a mouthful of ham and pineapple.

Up to this point there hadn't been much conversation flowing. More like the awkward silence of kids traumatized by the absence of their smartphones. We had no screens to hide behind. The concept of face-to-face time, without the actual use of FaceTime, was as unfamiliar as it was uncomfortable.

I shot a quick look around the room. In addition to the kids who'd arrived with me, there were already several others hanging out.

The guy persisted. "Yeah, I'm talking to you, girl. You got a name?" He studied my face, then spoke to the guy sitting beside him. "What do you think, Scott? I say she looks like a Moonbeam, or a Sky, or something all-natural-granola, right? That pale skin, that dark hair. Those eyes." He didn't wait for Scott's answer, turning to me again. "So what is it? Starchild?"

My lips twisted as I anticipated his reaction. "Raven."

"Ha! I knew it." He bumped shoulders with his friend. "Girl's named after a bird. Did I call that or what?"

"You called it, Milo," Scott said.

"Now that we've been formally introduced"—Milo smiled through residual bits of melted cheese stuck in his teeth—"I'll ask you one more time, Raven, what's your deal? General anxiety? Social anxiety? You don't seem like the agoraphobia type. Those ones are never so calm, usually screaming their heads off by now."

"You seem to know how this goes down." I struggled for a tone of casual interest. It wouldn't be smart to start asking a million pointed questions. "Have you been part of this trial before? They don't let you do that, do they? Repeat the same one over and over?"

Scott answered this time. "Sure they do. Why would they turn away the likes of us? We're textbook subjects. Plus the payout is too good to not come back. Free room. Netflix. A nice bit of cash on your way out the door. A warning though. You can't book another visit to the good doctor until you've been out of the trial for at least a week. Drugs gotta leave your system. They like clean slates. You might want to think on that if you're planning another stay."

While Milo filled me in on the benefits of participating multiple times in this obviously illegal drug trial, I scouted the place like I would any other target location. At either end of the hall stood men in lab coats, their arms crossed. I supposed they were aiming for the "official medical staff" look, but the bulging muscles threatening to rip those lab coats at the seams, and their carefully blank expressions, pretty much screamed "security detail." There weren't any windows.

"What you thinking, girl? You changed your mind and want to head home?" Milo shook his head. "Not going to happen. Once you sign on the dotted line, there's only one way out. In three days. When the trial's over." He shot Scott an amused grin. "Maybe she's one of those claustrophobes." He eyed me. "Walls closing in yet, Raven? Getting hard to breathe? Wishing you could fly on out of here?"

As he spoke, I felt a distinctly physical reaction. The walls did seem to be pressing in on me. I had to work at bringing air into my lungs. What the hell? Was Milo some sort of hypnotist?

I gripped the edge of my chair, my stomach churning.

A featherlight touch on my arm had me spinning like I'd been grabbed and whirled around. "What the hell do you want?" I glared at the younger girl who'd come to stand beside me. She didn't say anything, just tugged on my sleeve, insistent. And it ticked me off. "Quit pawing at me." I stood, towering over her much-shorter frame. "You want something, kid? Use your words before I dig them out of your throat for you."

She held her hands up in surrender.

Milo and Scott laughed.

"Telling the mute to *use your words*," Milo echoed. "That's priceless."

I sucked in a breath, studied the girl's face, noticed the panic and concern. *Rats.* She'd only been trying to help me get away from the two goons, and I'd scared the crap out of her. Plus—apparently she couldn't speak.

"Sorry, kid." I spoke louder than normal and shoved my chair back under the table. I held out my hands and moved them to my chest, faking an attempt at sign language. "You need something?"

The girl pulled a small notebook and pen out of her hoodie pocket. She scribbled for a bit, then angled the page so I could see what she'd written.

I'm Emma. I don't speak. Ever. I'm not deaf, so don't insult me with the loud speaking and hand motions. You should meet the rest of the girls and stay away from those asshats. Trust me, we're way cooler.

She gestured to another table where a few girls sat, looking at me expectantly. I glanced between Emma, the girls and Milo and Scott. It was no contest. I followed Emma across the room.

"Typical. Girls rule, boys drool, right, Raven?" Milo threw at my back.

"You called it again, Milo," I said, making Scott snort even as Milo slapped him in the back of the head.

The girls observed me silently as I sat at their table. Oh lordy, were they all mute?

"So…" I said awkwardly. "Don't everyone talk at once."

One of them laughed. "Don't worry. Emma's the only one who won't talk your ear off. She's got what they like to call selective mutism, but I think she's just super picky about who she lets into the inner circle. I respect that, you know what I mean?"

I gave a slow nod.

"We weren't going to step in, but Emma said no one should spend time with Milo and Scott if they don't have to. She's right. I'm Leena, by the way."

"Well, thanks. Raven." I held out my hand. "They seemed cool at first."

"Yeah, so does a tornado until you're dead in the wreckage."

"All right, everyone," Dr. Millie said, coming into the dining area. "It's time to move out."

"Move out?" I mumbled under my breath. "Out where?"

Leena shook her head. "What did you think, we were going to sleep here on the floor?" She laughed. "We're not that barbaric."

Oh, really? That's probably not what the dead kids would say.

SIXTEEN

"Come on, Raven, it won't be as bad as all that. I promise. You've been dosed twice already anyway," Millie explained with a patient smile that looked more like a smirk. Like she was enjoying my unease.

Twice? What was she talking about?

She must have seen the confusion in my eyes. "You think we take just anyone on our trial? We screen out the weakest links, Raven. Remember the water you drank? The tongue swabs we took? You have all already been given small quantities of Ally to check for potential allergic reactions."

Holy hell, that meant I could already be experiencing some of the side effects? I wasn't feeling suicidal, but I *had* been seeing things. I flashed back to Ryan's face, gasping for breath, even though he had clearly been deader than dead. And the walls closing in earlier. My pulse pounded out of control. What else wasn't real?

"Hold her still."

I jerked forward, but not fast enough to evade Simon's grip. He pulled me to his chest, his muscular arm braced against my throat. The force of his movement had us crashing into a wall-mounted medicine cabinet. Pill bottles rattled inside.

"Ugh, these kids are such a pain in my ass." Millie ignored my struggles as I clawed at Simon's chokehold. She calmly plucked a key from the many dangling from a lanyard around her neck, opened the glass door and righted the bottles.

Nostrils flaring, I desperately dragged air into my lungs while keeping my teeth clenched tight.

His arm compressed my windpipe. I needed to breathe. Now.

My mouth opened and I sucked at the air with ragged gulps.

Millie took full advantage. Shoving two blue pills into my mouth, she slammed my jaw shut. Simon eased off a bit. I could breathe through my nose finally, but now the problem wasn't getting air into my lungs—it was keeping the pills from slipping down my throat.

"Take all the time you need," Millie said, keeping steady pressure on my jaw. "You'll have to swallow eventually. The average person swallows twice a minute when awake, so we'll just wait you out."

I'd never felt such rage. I'd never been so powerless.

My worst nightmare was coming true. I'd never wanted to be like them, but I was losing the fight. Giving in. Slipping away.

My last conscious thought—soon I'd be a monster too.

SEVENTEEN

I woke up back in my room with zero idea how I'd gotten there. I swiped a bit of drool off my chin. I must have been totally out of it to crash so hard. Could have been the drugs, could have been a result of the crazed panic I'd felt when the drugs started to kick in. That definitely hadn't just been the trial drug. They must have dosed me with a tranquilizer.

I staggered to my feet. The room tilted fun-house style as I took the few steps to the door. I twisted the doorknob, but it didn't budge. They had locked me in. I knew that should tick me off. I should be raging at the world. Hell-bent on revenge. Retribution.

That's what I did. What I was.

But my head was a mess. I couldn't think straight. My knees bashed into the edge of the bed. Hell, I couldn't even walk in a straight line.

Everything and everyone around me was crooked.

I didn't deserve any better. Anything honest or good.

Didn't deserve Emmett.

Or the team.

I would only hurt them in the end. The monsters were right. I was just like them, and there was only one thing left to do. Make it stop.

Time shifted. I slammed a chair against the bedroom window. *Why am I doing that?* Glass exploded across the floor. Cool wind sucked my breath away.

I jumped, but it wasn't enough. I didn't die. I didn't break.

So I ran.

The road rose to meet my steps.

I blinked, and all was still. My body, unmoving. Darkness surrounding me. I blinked again and I was charging full out, arms pumping at my sides, heart hammering in my ears. Lungs burning.

I can feel them. Closer with each panicked breath. The monsters were back, and I wasn't sure they had ever left.

Streetlights flickered. *Or is that lightning? Or is the moon laughing down at me? Leaving me to my fate?*

I squinted into the sharp light, shielding my eyes with a trembling hand. Horrific faces danced into view. Rotting flesh. Blackened teeth that snapped and bit out words I didn't understand.

I'm not the girl who cries! But still a sob clawed up my throat.

The monsters are many. They're hungry. And they know my name.

"Ravvennn…"

"Ravvvveeennn…"

No, not again. Never again.

The sob became a scream that singed my lips like it was on fire.

EIGHTEEN

A nauseating scent filled my nostrils, and I awoke on a gasp. I tried to plug my nose, but my hand struck a mix of canvas and rubber. I opened my eyes to see Jace waving his shoe around.

"Are you trying to kill me?" I groaned. "Oh, man. That's disgusting."

"I told you my workout Chucks would do the trick." Jace grinned at Jo and Bentley, also hovering too close for comfort.

I struggled to sit up, shoving away the hands that dove in to help. "I'm all right, already. Back off or face the consequences. And by that, I mean you die."

Jo laughed. "Glad to have you kinda sorta back to normal. Although…I never really understood the expression *death warmed over* until now." Her eyes narrowed. "You don't look so good, Raven. How do you feel?"

Like I'd barely managed to crawl out of my own personal hell. Not that I wanted to go into the details. "I'm good." Over Jo's disbelieving snort, I continued. "Or I will be once you guys tell me how you found me." I scowled at Bentley. "Did you inject me with a tracker or something when I wasn't looking?"

Jace dropped his shoe to the floor and worked his foot back inside. "Much as Bentley would like to take the credit, you should know we'd be the last people to perform any kind of medical procedure on you without your say-so."

I swallowed down a rush of guilt. Jace was right. Their father had done that and more to Bentley for years. It just wasn't in them to be anything like their dad.

"It was Jonathan McNair, the kid you saved from his health-food-crazy stepmother," Jo said, breaking the very loud silence that had settled in the room. "He texted Bentley to say he'd found you stumbling around the theater district, busting up a red-carpet event. Some horror-movie premiere with a bunch of actors and fans in crazy costumes."

"It was a video-game launch, and the fans were cosplaying," Bentley corrected.

"Riighht," Jo drawled. "Anyway, apparently you were babbling about monsters and screaming your lungs out until Jonathan and his girlfriend managed to corral you away from the crowd. Then you passed out. He called Bent, and Bent sent Jace and me to get you."

"How long was I out?"

"Not long—an hour, tops." Jo's gaze was sympathetic. "What happened? Why the radio silence? We sent you a billion texts, did check-ins at the center off and on all day, but there was zero activity."

I shook my head. "That's because we weren't there. They took our phones, drove us to this old Victorian house in the old part of town." My skull pounded. "I thought it would be easy to avoid getting dosed, but they'd gotten to us already."

"What? When?" Jace's jaw clenched.

I filled them in as much as I could, and by the time I was finished, the air was charged with frustration and anger.

"Worst part? I freaked out and bolted. There are at least ten other kids still in that house. And they're all slated to get another round of meds tomorrow. We have to get them out of there before…"

"We'll do our best, Raven, you know we will," Jo said. "We just need to pinpoint the location. You didn't recognize any landmarks?"

"The bus windows were blacked out, so we couldn't see a thing. But I figure we drove for about half an hour before we arrived at the house." I shot Bentley

117

a look. "And it's obviously within jogging distance of the theater district. Gives us a ballpark, right?"

He smiled. "Sure, but we can do better than that. If they didn't confiscate your burner at the house, I can trace its exact location."

I frowned. "So you *did* have a tracker on me."

Jo nudged my shoulder. "But not through a nasty injection."

Bentley tapped on his keyboard. He turned the laptop so we could see the map on the monitor. He zoomed in on a crosshatch of streets. "Got it. The burner is on and hasn't moved for the last six hours. It's there in the house. On Richards Street."

"Let's go get those kids." I shoved up onto my feet. Jo kept me steady.

"We bust them out and then what? Bring possibly tripping kids back here until the drug wears off?" Jace asked.

"Great plan." I nodded. "Let's do it."

"No, no, no…forget I said anything." He held up his hands in surrender.

"I have to agree with Jace," Bentley said. "The best thing would be for them to go to the hospital in case there are any complications." His fingers once again flew over his keyboard. "I can hack the city's main gas-line regulator system and set off a false gas-leak alarm. The gas company responds quickly to those, along with the fire department." He nodded at his screen. "There should be several units at the house in a matter of minutes. They'll have to investigate and will need access to the house. That, along with the anonymous tip I'm sending to the police, should ensure the kids are taken into care safely."

I bit my lip. "Bentley, I have to warn you. Emmett's dad told me the police are very interested in you and your…let's call it *specialized skill set*. What if they track you because of that tip?"

Bentley grinned, looking very much like his older brother at that moment. "Let them try." He glanced at Jace. "I may not fight in the ring, but I know how to dodge and weave better than he can."

"I sure hope so."

NINETEEN

"Remind me again why you thought putting me in a monkey suit would be more fun than my family barbecue?" Emmett pulled awkwardly at his paisley tie.

I grinned. "You were the one who wanted to *help the team out in any way you could*. This is you. *Coulding.*" He really did look uncomfortable. And nervous. It wasn't every day you got dragged into a plot to take down a pharmaceutical company worth millions.

And if this didn't play out the way we expected, the team was staring down the barrel of some serious payback.

My smile faded. "You know, you don't have to…"

Emmett touched a finger to my lips. "Stop right there. I'm in, Raven." His gaze held mine. "I'm all in."

"Enough, please—some things you can't unhear." A voice blasted through the inner-ear comm devices Bentley had set us up with earlier.

"Get bent, Bent," I hissed, flushing and pulling away from Emmett. He didn't let me get far, though, looping my arm through his and guiding me into the ballroom.

A snooty attendant stopped us at the double-door entrance. "Invitation, please."

Emmett handed over the gold-trimmed card that Jace had rooted through his father's mail to uncover and which Jo had altered to include our names.

"You two are press?" The attendant studied the invitation, then gave us the once-over.

"That's right," Emmett said with confidence. "We're bloggers for the Health and Wellness Network." He gave a self-deprecating smile. "This is the first time they've sent us to cover an event of this size. Let's hope we don't screw it up."

I elbowed him. "Speak for yourself, King of the Typos. Remember the time you got that heart surgeon's name wrong? What did you call him? Doctor Death?" I laughed, maybe a little too loudly.

Emmett grimaced. "Rotten autocorrect. It was supposed to be Doctor *Heath*. Not my fault that's not a common-enough name to make it into my cell phone's dictionary."

I snorted. "You shouldn't be composing a press release on your phone…"

A lineup had started to form behind us. The attendant gave a disinterested nod and moved us along.

We were in. The warm lighting danced off the flashy sequined dresses worn by most of the women in attendance, myself included. Emmett wasn't the only one who was playing dress-up. I held my head high. We might not be as rich as these people, or as educated, or entitled, but at least we were doing what we could to protect the little guy. The average person.

Not people so glossed up with makeup and Botox and hair product they didn't look real.

"*Doctor Death*?" Emmett said. "Nice bit of improv."

"You weren't too bad yourself. Way to keep up." A shiver ran through me as our shoulders brushed and I became very aware of how tall Emmett was. How strong. How much I wanted to lean into that strength.

My heart pounded in my chest.

"Children, if we can stay focused on the task at hand," Bentley said, making both of us jump. "Your target is approaching the stage."

Showtime.

TWENTY

The room dazzled. Light glinted from ornate crystal chandeliers and stained-glass windows. The restaurant was a converted bank that had been restored to its former Victorian glory. They'd even kept the impressive brass-and-steel vault door. A glance at the lock had my fingers itching to give the combination a go. Safecracking was a skill I'd always wanted to develop further, and these old beauties were built to outlast us all.

"Ladies and gentlemen, colleagues and members of the press, welcome to the opening keynote address of the

Pharmaceutical Development Association's twelfth annual conference."

A round of applause from the audience.

"We're lucky to have one of the country's foremost minds with us to share her insights into the issue of anxiety and today's youth." The lights dimmed further. Emmett and I steadily wove through tables and clusters of people until we found our table and the two empty chairs waiting for us.

Well done on Jace's part. We were only a few feet from the stage and had a clear line of sight to Dr. Millie as she stood at the podium.

"Thank you so much. Let's dive right in, shall we?" A large projection screen lowered behind her. "As most of you in this room are aware, there's been a marked increase in cases of teen anxiety since it was initially noticed in the early 1980s…" Photographs and infographics illustrated the points she made in her speech.

Her words droned on.

"Half of those statistics are taken out of context," Bentley said in my ear. "The way she's phrasing things, the omissions of crucial information…"

"And they're eating it up." Emmett sat down and observed the crowd.

"Ugh, she's a piece of work." Bentley's frustration came through the in-ear monitors loud and clear.

"She certainly is." The words croaked out of my mouth. It took everything I had to stay seated when I just wanted to get up and punch that woman in the throat. No wonder Jace had taken up boxing. I was beginning to see the appeal.

"You okay?" Emmett shot me a worried glance.

"I will be once we take her down."

"Don't do anything yet," Bentley said. "We're having trouble with the live feed from Jo's end."

"Get it fixed, Bent, or I can't make any promises."

My rage continued to build. I wanted to challenge every smug word leaving Dr. Millie's lips. Muscles in my legs tensed. The team had better pull through, or I was going to have to confront her on my own.

"Easy, Raven." Emmett put his hand over mine, making me aware that I'd been clutching at him, digging my nails into his thigh. "It will happen."

"Yeah, 'cause it's going to happen right now."

"Wait, Raven," Bentley and Emmett said, but I was already on my feet, waving my hands in the air. The crowd took notice. Dr. Millie kept her expression open and welcoming as she nodded my way.

"It appears we have excited you all so much that some of you can't wait for the Q&A." She laughed.

A spotlight shifted in my direction. Emmett tugged at my hand, but I was full steam ahead.

"Thanks so much, Dr. Millie," I gushed. "I'm so sorry to interrupt, but this is my first time covering an event for the Health and Wellness Network, and I'm just so excited to be here."

Millie squinted, her expression tolerant, but I could tell she was trying to see me better through the blinding lights. "Such enthusiasm is not to be faulted. What's your question, young lady?"

"I know our followers will be keen to hear more about the recent drug trials you've been conducting in our area. The ones for AL28-9, the drug you're planning to market to the masses under the name ALLY?"

"I'm sorry, my dear, but I'm afraid you're misinformed. I am not aware of any registered trials for that particular drug."

"Of course not. I'm not talking about legal trials. I mean the ones you've been conducting illegally on minors without their parents' informed consent." I smiled, ignoring the grumblings from the people around me.

Emmett stood at my side, glaring at the security guards coming up the side of the room. "We've got company."

"Bentley…" I mumbled under my breath.

"I got you—we're good from this end. Give me a minute to remote-access her laptop, but we're going to have a good long talk later about jumping the gun."

I tilted my chin down and made a show of digging through my clutch for a small notebook. "Whatever you say, Bentley. Just work your magic, wizard." I held the notebook high and addressed the crowd. "I have proof, right here. Firsthand accounts from seven test subjects. Students who attend public schools in this very city."

The doctor scoffed. "What is this, some sort of prank for your YouTube channel? I'll bet you're not even a Health and Wellness blogger."

"It's go time," Bentley said.

I let my smile widen. "Probably the first correct diagnosis you've made in a while."

"Where's security? Get her out of here."

Just then the screen behind the doctor flickered. Feedback squealed through the loudspeakers. Everyone faced the screen. Millie paled.

"Do you recognize that café, Dr. Millie?" I asked. "What about the girl sitting at the corner table?"

"That's…that's my daughter," the doctor sputtered. "What the…?"

"You've said you're confident in Ally's ability to treat teens with anxiety. And that it will easily pass all FDA and Health Canada testing. You're so confident you've been secretly testing teens across the city including at least three who have killed themselves. Well, why don't we put your faith to the test. If there are no adverse side effects, then you wouldn't mind if your daughter was one of the test subjects, would you?"

The screen blackened, then flickered back to life, drawing everyone's stare. I knew it was Jace behind the phone camera, filming in real time as Jo entered the frame. She was dressed as a barista, the café's apron around her waist, and wore an angled-bob wig with the hair strategically blocking her face. She expertly prepared a latte, flashed a pill at the camera and then dropped it into the steaming drink.

"No, don't do this—this can't be happening…" Millie said, her mic picking up the panic in her voice.

The camera followed Jo as she glided across the café, set the drink on the young woman's table and walked away.

"No, Katie, don't drink it, noooo!" Millie screamed, her voice echoing in the silent ballroom.

The crowd gasped as the girl took one sip, then another. The screen went dark.

"What have you done?" Millie asked, hunched over the podium, barely able to stand.

I felt for her then, but I didn't want to. I looked away to see two forms taking shape in my peripheral vision. My parents, standing there in the crowd. Unlike everyone else, they weren't looking at the screen or the podium, but glaring right at me. Like they wanted to rip me to pieces.

A wail of despair from the stage had me snapping my head around. *Forget them—they aren't here.* The real monster was up on that stage.

"No, Doctor. What have *you* done?" I said. The screen came to life once more.

Two guards suddenly grabbed Emmett and brought him under control, snapping his arms behind his back and fixing them in place with plastic ties.

Photos of kids flashed across the screen, pictures Bentley had copied from their Facebook pages. "These are the daughters and sons you've killed."

I held out my hands for the guard to take me in without a fight, but I kept yelling out the accusations, knowing the crowd was listening. Judging. "They're all test subjects of your illegal trial. All of them committed suicide within forty-eight hours of your trial dosages. How do you think your daughter will handle it?"

The security guards shoved us from the room, and the audience exploded into shouts as the double doors slammed shut.

TWENTY-ONE

Officer Daniels met us at the rear entrance. He did not look pleased. I took a step closer to Emmett, not sure if I was offering him my support or needing some myself. The guards were having none of it either way, jerking us both in opposite directions.

When I stumbled under the rough handling, Officer Daniels's eyes narrowed even more. "I'll take it from here, boys."

The guards handed us over and strode back toward the conference room, now beginning to empty in a steady stream of outraged delegates.

"Dad, you came," Emmett started, but his father cut him off with a curt shake of his head.

"Not here."

We walked silently across the foyer and outside to his police cruiser. Daniels opened the back door, and we awkwardly climbed in. Even the smallest action is ten times harder with your hands tied behind your back. He tossed us a pair of wire clippers.

"Figure that out amongst yourselves."

"Here, let me." Ever the gentleman, Emmett worked the clippers, setting me free first. It took a bit of contortion work from both of us, but he eventually sliced through the plastic without slicing through me. With my hands free, I took a second to remove Emmett's comm link from his ear and pocketed it, ignoring the disappointment in his gaze, and then snipped the plastic ties around his wrists. I rubbed at the itch and irritation already starting on my own wrists.

"Where can I drop you off, Raven?" Daniels said.

I hesitated. Even Emmett didn't know where I lived or anything about *Big Daddy*.

"At the corner is fine. I can make my way from there."

"Raven." Disappointment rang in Emmett's voice. "We can give you a ride home, you know. We don't care where you live—we're not going to use that information against you. We just want you home safe." He sighed. "After everything, you really don't trust us?"

My mouth opened, but the words Emmett wanted refused to leave my lips. Did I trust them? Yes, to a certain extent. But I didn't even feel comfortable with Jo knowing where I laid my head, let alone a cop who might have a change of heart and decide to turn me in if things got sticky for him down the road.

"No, it's better this way, Emmett." Daniels met my gaze in the rearview mirror.

"If my boss asks, I can't tell him what I don't know. I just have one question. Did you really dose that girl?"

I shook my head hard. "No way." They had to understand. "We'd never hurt anyone like that. It was just some mints. We were all about shock and awe, not actually out to do damage."

"That's good, Raven," Daniels said. "You have to be careful you don't take things too far."

"Like the doctor did?"

"You better hope no one was filming that debacle. If you show up on TV screens or the Internet, I won't be able to protect you from the repercussions."

"Not to worry, Officer Daniels. We factored in every contingency."

His eyes narrowed. "Your tech guy is that good?"

"Yeah, he is. A true wizard."

He shot Emmett a dark look. "This isn't going to end well, son. Eventually this team is going to get in over their heads and get caught. I don't want you involved when they do."

"I never wanted Emmett to get in trouble. I won't put him at risk. Not anymore." I swallowed hard. "We're agreed on that."

"No," Emmett growled. "We're not. If you need me, Raven, I'm there. No questions asked."

He was dead serious. I sat there, staring at Emmett. He was trying to be so strong as he stood up to his dad, taking a stance against him—for me. He didn't get how lucky he was to have a dad who had his back, someone to keep the monsters at bay. Which was why I had to let him go. Once and for all.

Because for me, the monsters were closing in. My lungs constricted.It was hard to breathe. I couldn't take it anymore.

"Pull over," I said. "Now."

Daniels drew to a stop. He got out of the car and held my door open, silent, letting me decide my next move.

"Raven," Emmett pleaded, "you can't just…"

But I was out the door and running down the darkened street into the night.

TWENTY-TWO

"Are you sure about this?" Bentley's fingers hovered over his keyboard.

Over the last few days I'd thought long and hard about how to deal with the Emmett situation. Though my stomach lurched at the knowledge that I'd likely never see him again, I knew a clean break was the best way to go.

"Do it."

And with those two little words I was officially no longer a student at Laurier Secondary. My data was wiped. It was like I'd never walked those halls. Hadn't kissed Emmett in the library.

Or sat shoulder to shoulder with him on the roof, watching the world slip by under our feet.

"Sorry it didn,'t work out, Raven." Jo gave me a cautious couple of pats on the back. She knew better than to try for a hug, but after the stress I'd been under lately, I might have accepted one.

We'd given each other some space after taking down Dr. Millie and her illegal drug trial. But Bentley had called us back in for a meeting. The team might have been having some downtime, but the emails from kids needing our help hadn't slowed down one bit.

I'd used the slow period to enlist Bentley's tech know-how to give me a change of pace.

New school.

New name.

"Thanks, Bent." I nudged him with my hip. "Much appreciated."

"You betcha."

I hoped it was enough to keep Emmett from finding me. I didn't know what I'd do if we came face-to-face. I wasn't sure I could look into his eyes and tell him I didn't need him anymore. I couldn't lie to him, which was why I'd had to sneak off like the criminal I was.

Jace took a swig of milk straight from the carton. "Does this mean Daniels is out of the picture too? We didn't break up with the cop just because we're ditching his kid, right?"

Jo, Bentley and I all shot glares his way.

"What?" Jace shrugged. "No disrespect to the death of true love. I'm just saying Daniels has been useful."

I swiped a hand across my forehead. A nasty throbbing had settled behind my eyes. "We can use Officer Daniels if necessary. I pretty much made a deal with him—he'll continue to help us as long as Emmett doesn't get dragged into things."

Jace looked over at Jo. "See. Raven knows I'm not being insensitive. That's all I wanted to know."

She rolled her eyes. "Oh yeah, you're all heart."

"You're good to go, Raven," Bentley interrupted. "I've registered you with a school across town, under the name you requested, Jane Smith."

Jace laughed. "That's original."

"It's boring and uninspired," I corrected, "and so obvious I'm sure Emmett will overlook it. If he tries to find me."

"Oh, he's going to come looking." Jace crushed the empty milk carton, then fired it into the sink. "That guy has it bad."

"And how would you know?" Jo smirked. "When have you had it bad?"

"I just know, okay?" Jace sputtered. "Why is this about me all of a sudden? Bentley, didn't you have a point for this meeting?"

"Right." Bentley shifted his laptop to face us. "First, the good news. Thanks to our latest efforts, Dr. Millie and her associates have been charged with conducting illegal drug trials."

"Yay!" Jo let out a little cheer.

"But the bad news…the pharmaceutical company she works for is still going strong. Their running statement is that Millie went rogue and they had no knowledge of her testing facility. They've wiped their hands of her and remain untouchable. The drug ALLY will probably be released within the next year or so, but under a new name."

"But Dr. Millie will never work in her field again," Jo offered. "That's a win."

"One step forward, two steps back," I said. My fists clenched, fingernails digging into my palms. "At least we managed to get that group of kids out of danger, and justice for the ones who died."

"Agreed," Bentley said, scrolling through emails. "Which brings me to the other kids needing some retribution. I think it's best if we screen the potentials together. Let's see…how do you guys feel about kids forced to work in a telemarketing scam, or one living with an abusive grandparent…wait, there's also a case of stolen identity." He paused. "No, routine." His eyes widened. "Maybe not."

I tuned him out. *Ugh.* So many messed-up lives. Sometimes it was overwhelming. How could our small team put a dent in the madness? It would be so easy to walk away, not just from Emmett, but from the team, from the kids who needed help to survive.

While Jo and Jace searched through the messages for their next case, I wandered over to the long line of windows at the far side of the kitchen. The sun had set, and the wide expanse of lawn outside was illuminated by a row of solar lights. They weaved toward a large outdoor pool. The water glittered, the surface shifting slightly with the breeze.

"Hey," Bentley said, standing at my side. "I know you said to stay out of it, but…" He handed me a flash drive.

"What's this?" The drive barely weighed an ounce but felt like lead in my hand.

"Everything you wanted to know about your parents and then some. Diesel lied to you, Raven, about so much." Bentley rested a hand on my arm. "The second you want to move on this, we'll be ready." Before I could blast him for interfering when I had expressly told him to stand down, he slipped back to the others.

I wanted to throw the drive across the room, trash it in the garbage or crunch it under my Docs. But I didn't do any of those things. I just stood there, barely breathing. My fingers folded over the drive, sealing it in my fist. This was why I couldn't walk away. Together we did make a difference. I was living proof.

Without the team, I'd be in a very dark place. Maybe even dead. The more kids we saved, the more wrongs we righted. The more those kids might stand up for someone else. Infinite possibilities.

Maybe big changes started with a few small actions.

"Raven, did we lose you?" Jo called.

"*Ravennn…where's our little bird?*" The monsters called too, but I'd deal with them later.

For the time being, I stuffed the drive in my back pocket and joined my team. We had work to do.

A NOTE TO READERS

Many young people experience anxiety, but for some, the worry and stress can be overwhelming and impact home and school life, relationships and employment.

Please remember that anxiety can be safely managed and treated. Don't let it get out of control.

And you don't have to deal with it on your own. Ask for help. Talk to an adult you trust. Or call the Kids Help Phone: 1-800-668-6868 (Canada). If you live in the United States call 1-800-273-TALK (8255).

ACKNOWLEDGMENTS

Many thanks to fellow Retribution authors Sigmund and Natasha for the great fun planning and plotting ways to torment our collective characters. Thanks also for the editing prowess of Tanya Trafford and the fantastic support of the staff at Orca. You are all so very wonderful.

JUDITH GRAVES is the author of several award-winning novels, including *Exposed*, her first installment in the Retribution series. She loves tragic romance, werewolves, vampires, magic and all things a bit creepy. A firm believer that teen fiction can be action-packed and snarky yet hit all the right emotional notes, Judith writes stories with attitude. She lives in northern Alberta. For more information, visit www.judithgraves.com.